For my goddaughter

Riley Ann

ANN ESTELLE STORIES

# QUEEN of HALLOWEEN

### BY MARY ENGELBREIT

HarperCollinsPublishers

nn Estelle had the perfect Halloween costume: a long lacy skirt, a bright shiny wand, and a pair of glittery wings. And a crown, of course. She was the Fairy Queen.

Her friend Michael was a pirate. He had a sword, an eye patch, and big black boots.

"Yo-ho-ho!" said Michael.

"Tra-la-la!" said Ann Estelle.

"Trick or treat!"

**W**e don't need a grown-up," said Michael. "We're old enough to go out trick-or-treating alone."

Ann Estelle wasn't sure about that. The night looked *very* dark. But she didn't want Michael to think she was scared.

ell, you might not need a grown-up, but I need some kids," said Ann Estelle's father. "Let's go, before all the candy's gone!"

**A**nn Estelle had been right. The night *was* dark. Even the streetlights didn't seem very bright.

There were ghosts and witches running everywhere.

"Don't be scared," said Ann Estelle's father, and he squeezed her hand tight. "It's just pretend."

"I know," said Ann Estelle. But she squeezed his hand back.

"Pirates are brave," said Michael.

"Queens are brave too," said Ann Estelle.

"I t's late," said Ann Estelle's father. "Time to head home."

"One more house," said Ann Estelle.

"And can we go alone?" asked Michael. "We're old enough!"

ll right," said Ann Estelle's father. "I'll wait for you on the sidewalk. Just go up and ring the doorbell."

T he house was big and old. The wind blew in the bushes as
Ann Estelle and Michael came up the sidewalk. The closer they got,
the scarier the house looked. They could hear a dog barking nearby.

Ann Estelle didn't like big dogs.

She wanted to look back at her dad. But then Michael would know **she was scared.**

**T**he porch steps creaked. The dog barked again.

"I don't think anybody's home," Michael whispered. "Let's go back."

Ann Estelle looked at Michael.

His voice sounded shaky.

he eye that wasn't covered by the patch was very wide.

Ann Estelle realized something.

*Michael* was afraid!

omehow that made Ann Estelle feel braver.

"Let's ring the bell," she said.

"But there's a dog!" said Michael.

"It's in the backyard," said Ann Estelle. "It won't hurt us."

he pushed the doorbell with her finger.

Nobody came.

"See, nobody's home," said Michael.

But then the door cracked open.

"Trick or treat!" said Ann Estelle. She poked Michael.

"Trick or treat!" he said.

"ou're my last trick-or-treaters," said the white-haired woman who opened the door. "So you might as well take **all** the candy."

ichael and Ann Estelle held out their bags. Then they ran down the front walk to Ann Estelle's father.

ou did it!" he said.

"Queens are brave," said Ann Estelle. "And pirates too."

 o you weren't even a little scared?" asked her father.

Ann Estelle looked at Michael. Michael looked at Ann Estelle.

"Oh, we were scared, all right!" Ann Estelle said. "But, you know, you have to be *a little scared* so you can be brave!"

Queen of Halloween

© 2008 by Mary Engelbreit Ink

Manufactured in China.

All rights reserved. No part of this book may be used or reproduced in any manner whatsoever without written permission except in the case of brief quotations embodied in critical articles and reviews. For information address HarperCollins Children's Books, a division of HarperCollins Publishers, 1350 Avenue of the Americas, New York, NY 10019.

www.harpercollinschildrens.com

Library of Congress Cataloging-in-Publication Data

Engelbreit, Mary.

Queen of Halloween / by Mary Engelbreit. — 1st ed.

p.   cm.   Summary: When Ann Estelle and her friend Michael go trick-or-treating and approach a big scary house, they both learn that courage means also being afraid.

ISBN 978-0-06-008190-4 (trade bdg.) — ISBN 978-0-06-008191-1 (lib. bdg.)

[1. Halloween—Fiction. 2. Fear—Fiction. 3. Courage—Fiction.] I. Title.

PZ7.E69975Qsh  2008   [E]—dc22   2007010894   CIP   AC

Typography by Stephanie Bart-Horvath

1 2 3 4 5 6 7 8 9 10

❖

First Edition